DATE DUE

JUL 1 8 2012			
AUG 0 7 2012			
MAR 0 9 2013			
	AUG 2 6 2013		

Demco, Inc. 38-293

KLOOZ
The Snarling Suspect

by J. Banscherus
translated by Daniel C. Baron
illustrated by Ralf Butschkow

Librarian Reviewer
Marci Peschke
Librarian, Dallas Independent School District
MA Education Reading Specialist, Stephen F. Austin State University
Learning Resources Endorsement, Texas Women's University

Reading Consultant
Sherry Klehr
Elementary/Middle School Educator, Edina Public Schools, MN
MA in Education, University of Minnesota

STONE ARCH BOOKS
Minneapolis   San Diego

First published in the United States in 2008
by Stone Arch Books, A Capstone Imprint
151 Good Counsel Drive, P.O. Box 669
Mankato, Minnesota 56002
www.capstonepub.com

First published by Arena Books
Rottendorfer str. 16, D-97074
Würzburg, Germany

Library of Congress Cataloging-in-Publication Data
Banscherus, Jürgen.
    [Hunde, Hüte, und Halunken. English.]
    The Snarling Suspect / by J. Banscherus; translated by Daniel C.
Baron; illustrated by Ralf Butschkow.
    p. cm. — (Klooz)
    "Pathway books."
    Summary: When his dog is falsely accused of attacking other dogs
and people, Bill the Mask asks Klooz to investigate.
    ISBN-13: 978-1-59889-875-0 (library binding)
    ISBN-10: 1-59889-875-2 (library binding)
    ISBN-13: 978-1-59889-911-5 (paperback)
    ISBN-10: 1-59889-911-2 (paperback)
    [1. Great Dane—Fiction. 2. Dogs—Fiction. 3. Mystery and detective
stories.] I. Baron, Daniel C. II. Butschkow, Ralf, ill. III. Title.
PZ7.B22927Sn 2008
[Fic]—dc22   2007006623

Art Director: Heather Kindseth
Graphic Designer: Kay Fraser

Printed in the United States of America in Stevens Point, Wisconsin.
072010
005869R

Table of contents

TOP SECRET

KLOOZ

The Snarling Suspect

CHAPTER 1

No Missing Dogs!

Last Saturday, the doorbell rang. It was Ms. Becker. She lives right above the apartment my mom and I live in.

"Sampson ran away!" she cried. "I don't know what to do. You have to help me, Klooz!"

Sampson is Ms. Becker's dog. He barks all the time.

Sometimes his barking is so loud that it keeps me and my mom up at night.

When that happens we wish we could glue his mouth shut.

I shook my head. "I'm sorry, Ms. Becker, but I don't find missing dogs."

"But why not?" she asked. "The police won't help me either!"

Of course not, I thought to myself.

They have better things to do with their time than to look for missing dogs.

Even though our neighbor begged for a while and offered me twenty dollars, I stood my ground.

If the other private detectives in the city found out that I was looking for lost dogs, I wouldn't be able to show my face in public anymore.

My detective career would be over.

Ms. Becker got her dog back after a few days. The little yapper was lost in the city park. Someone found him. Ms. Becker's phone number was on his collar, so he was returned home safely.

I don't look for dogs. No way!

That doesn't rule out cases involving dogs, though. Not anymore.

My last case had to do with a dog.

In fact, it was a very special dog.

After I had lost a detectives' contest a while ago, I had thought about ending my career as a private detective.

In the contest, I had lost so quickly. It was horrible.

I asked myself seriously if I wanted to keep working nights, being kidnapped, and lured into traps.

For advice, I visited Olga, one of my best friends. She owns the newspaper stand where I go to buy my Carpenter's chewing gum.

Olga tried to comfort me. "To me you are and will always be the greatest!" she said. "It doesn't matter if other detectives come along."

Usually Olga made me feel better. Today, her kind words didn't help.

Then one day, I met Bill the Mask.

I was sitting behind Olga's newspaper stand reading a magazine when I heard a deep growl. It sounded a lot like a motorcycle.

Curious, I stood up and peered around the corner of the newspaper stand.

I found myself eye to eye with a terrible monster.

It had huge yellow eyes, a gigantic dark nose, and a big mouth with two rows of huge teeth.

My heart stopped beating for a few seconds. It started to beat again when a man's deep voice said, "Come here, Odin. Be good!"

Then the monster turned around.

I saw that it was a Great Dane.

It was as big as a calf and had a
smooth gray coat.

Its owner was just as weird as the dog.

He was at least six feet tall and wore a big hat over his white hair.

The weirdest thing was the mask he wore between his eyes and his mouth. Halloween was still a long time away.

Why in the world was he wearing a mask on a normal day?

"You don't have to be afraid," he said. "Odin likes children."

Then he turned to Olga and said, "I need chocolate bars, please."

Olga put a few candy bars on the counter and introduced me to the man.

"This is Bill," she said.

"Everyone calls me Bill the Mask," the man said.

He laughed. "I lost my nose in a motorcycle accident. It's too bad. It was a good nose. Without the mask I look pretty horrible. What's your name?"

"Klooz," I answered.

"He's a private detective," Olga added.

"I'll take these chocolates," Bill the Mask said. "Let me have ten of them."

Then he turned to me. "So, you're a private detective?" he asked seriously.

I could hardly believe it. He sounded like he meant it. He wasn't laughing.

Bill the Mask was the first grown-up besides Olga who hadn't made fun of me for being a young private detective.

In spite of his weird mask, I liked him right away.

"Yes," I said. "Well, I was until a couple of weeks ago."

Bill the Mask pulled a crumpled piece of paper out of his jacket pocket and gave it to me.

"Read that, Klooz," he said.

"This is a ticket from the police,"
I said.

I looked at the paper and read more.
"It says on the 14th of this month your
dog injured another dog so badly that it
had to go to the vet."

I took a breath. Was this dog a killer?

I glanced at Bill the Mask and went
on, "In addition to
that, it has been
reported that your
dog illegally chases
rabbits and deer
in the city park.
You are ordered to
appear in person at
the police station,
room 234."

"My dog doesn't chase rabbits and deer in the park," Bill the Mask said. "He likes little dogs. Somebody wants to put me in a frying pan and turn up the heat."

In the pan!

"Maybe it's a mix-up," Olga suggested.

The man shook his head. "There aren't many dogs like Odin. Do you want to take the case, Klooz?"

"Do it, sweetie," Olga said, even though I had asked her not to call me that when other people were around.

I was interested in the case. Very
interested. It was a thinking man's
case. I wouldn't need fancy tools like a
computer or a cell phone. I would just
need my brain. I felt like my brain was
up for the challenge.

"Okay," I said. "I'll do it."

"What is your fee?" Bill the Mask
asked.

"When I solve the case, I get five
packs of Carpenter's chewing gum,"
I replied.

The man smiled. "You have good taste, kid. Carpenter's is the best gum."

He gave me his gigantic hand to shake. "It's a deal, Klooz," he said.

"Okay," I said. We shook on it.

I had no idea what Odin thought. The dog laid his huge paws on my shoulders and licked me across my face.

"EEEEEWWWWW!" I screamed and ran away. Olga and Bill the Mask laughed.

CHAPTER 2

The Case Begins

The next day, right after school, I started my search. I got Bill the Mask's address from Olga. Then I went to his house and waited for him and Odin to come outside.

I wanted to see with my own eyes how Odin behaved. I wasn't completely sure that the Great Dane with the motorcycle growl was as friendly and peaceful as his owner said he was.

When Bill and his dog finally came outside, I followed them to the park. Odin was pulling like crazy on his leash. It took all of Bill the Mask's strength to hold on to him.

Finally once they were in the park, Bill the Mask let his dog off the leash. I quickly looked for a large tree that I could climb if Odin found me.

The dog wasn't interested in finding me. He disappeared into the trees. Soon, he returned with a huge tree branch for his owner, dropped it at his feet, and disappeared again.

For the next half an hour the dog did nothing except bring tree branches and trunks for Bill the Mask. He seemed to have no interest in chasing deer or rabbits.

After a while, Bill the Mask put Odin back on his leash and headed home. I stayed hidden for a few minutes. Then I caught up with them at the park's parking lot.

"Hello, Klooz," Bill the Mask said with surprise. Odin started growling. "What are you doing?" Bill the Mask asked me.

"Oh, I just happened to be in the park," I replied.

Bill the Mask laughed and said, "You were following us, right? You wanted to know if Odin really bothered animals in the park, right?"

I nodded.

"You are pretty suspicious, Klooz. I like that. Every good detective is suspicious," Bill the Mask said.

"What happened at the police station?" I asked.

Bill the Mask petted his dog. "They dropped the case, but they also said they'd take Odin away if he was caught chasing animals in the park!" he said.

Then the dog walked over to me.

"You can pet him," Bill the Mask said.

He added, "Odin just wants to play. He is still just a puppy, you know. He's still growing."

"Gr . . . gr . . . growing? I see," I stuttered.

I carefully stuck my hand out and put it on the giant dog's fur. It felt nice!

"Odin likes you," Bill the Mask said. "He likes it when you pet him."

Almost as if on command, the dog tried to lick my face, just like the day before.

This time I was ready. I jumped backward. That morning, I had washed my face. I didn't want to have to do it again.

"You seem to think it wasn't a mix-up," I said. "There have to be other Great Danes in the city."

Bill the Mask shook his head. "I know them all. They are smaller than Odin, or their coat is a different color. Believe me, Klooz, somebody is out to get me."

"It seems like it," I mumbled. I stuck a piece of Carpenter's gum in my mouth. "Would you like a piece?" I asked Bill the Mask.

"Carpenter's? Of course! Now what happens?" he asked after he had taken a piece of gum. "I don't want anything to happen to my dog."

"I'll think of something," I replied.

On the way home from the park, I saw two Great Danes. One had a white coat and was pretty small. The other was as big as Odin, but its coat was almost all black.

No, it had not been a mix-up, I decided.

What should I do next?

Maybe I should put an ad in
the paper.

Who has it in for Odin and
Bill the Mask??????? Please call
Klooz at 555-8855.

No! That was a terrible idea.

I had to ask the man with the mask
if he had enemies. Maybe his neighbors
didn't like Odin. If that was a dead end, I
didn't know where I would look.

When I got home, the look on my
mom's face was not very happy.

"We agreed that you would come
home right away after school," she said.

"I know, Mom," I said.

"Have you done your homework?" she asked.

"I'll start doing it right away, Mom," I said.

She sighed and tousled my hair. "I just don't have enough time for you. My work at the hospital is making me crazy," Mom said.

"I love you, Mom," I said.

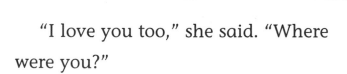

"I love you too," she said. "Where were you?"

"At the park," I replied.

"Were you working on a new case?" she asked, narrowing her eyes.

I nodded.

"I thought you were done with that," she began.

I interrupted her right away. "It's about a dog," I explained. I told her the story of Bill the Mask and Odin. My mom loves most dogs. I knew she would understand how important my case was.

I was right. "There are awful people in the world," she said when my story was done. "Will you solve the case?"

"Of course, Mom."

"How about ordering some pizza for dinner tonight?" she asked.

"Great idea!" I said.

CHAPTER 3

A Newspaper Surprise

That night I didn't sleep very well. I kept dreaming about gigantic dogs that were chasing me. They all had creepy yellow eyes.

The next morning I discovered that I was out of Carpenter's gum.

My mom had the early shift at the hospital, so I could eat whatever I wanted for breakfast.

I ate a slice of toast and had a glass of soda, which was usually strictly forbidden. Then I ran to Olga's.

"Good morning, my angel," Olga greeted me.

I can't get her to quit calling me things like that, no matter what I do. She always says she wishes she was my mom. That's why she thinks she has the right to call me "sweetie," "angel," and "darling."

"Hello, Olga," I said. "I need five packs of Carpenter's gum, please."

She pushed the gum across the counter. "Don't you ever get sick of this stuff?" she asked.

"Never," I replied. I started to leave.

Olga stopped me and pushed a newspaper into my hand. "This is today's paper," she said. "Read this article here."

"I don't have time, Olga," I said. "I have to go to school."

"Then take the newspaper with you," she said.

As I walked down Main Street I looked at the article.

The headline said "Great Dane Injures Walker."

> Yesterday afternoon at 3 p.m.,
> a 60-year-old walker was attacked
> by a stray dog. The injured man
> had to be taken to the hospital
> for treatment. According to the
> victim, the dog was an unusually
> large Great Dane with a gray coat.
> The dog seems to have disappeared
> without a trace.

That was supposed to have happened yesterday afternoon at three o'clock?

That was impossible.

Yesterday afternoon I was with Odin and Bill the Mask in the park.

I am sure that I would have noticed if Odin had bitten someone. I was there the whole time!

I couldn't concentrate on school that morning. I just kept thinking about the newspaper article, and about Odin.

It was the first time I got a bad grade in geography class.

How can a detective pay attention to geography when he is working on a puzzling case?

When I got home from school later that day, my mom was in the kitchen. She was making potatoes and sausages. That is one of my favorite meals.

I held the newspaper article in front of her face.

"You've got to read this," I said.

She read the article. "Do you think it was Odin?" she asked.

I shook my head. "I think I would have noticed."

Then I had an interesting thought. It might be a crazy idea, but I had to try it.

"I need your help, Mom," I said.

"Help with what?" she asked.

Two minutes later, Mom had the telephone in her hand.

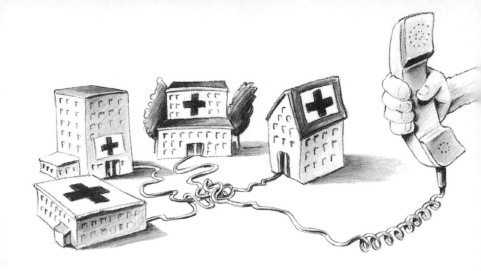

My mom called the four hospitals in the city. She knows nurses at all of them and all of the nurses were more than happy to help her.

What she learned from the phone calls was shocking: no one with a dog bite was treated at any of the hospitals.

"That is weird," Mom mumbled as she wiped sweat from her brow.

I took the phone from her hand, hung it up, and said, "Someone told the newspaper a lie. I've got to go."

"To the newspaper?" she yelled.

"Of course!" I called back.

At first the secretary at the newspaper didn't want to let me in.

When I made up a story about a mean dog and my poor cat, the secretary gave in.

She brought me to the man who had written the story about the person who was bitten.

The reporter was sitting in front of his computer. There were papers and photos spread all over his desk.

It reminded me a little of my bedroom at home.

"Yes?" the man asked without looking up from his computer screen.

"I want to talk to you about the man who was bitten by the Great Dane," I said. "Your story isn't true."

The reporter looked at me. "What's the matter with you?" he replied. "Of course it's true!"

"No it isn't," I replied quietly. I told him what my mom had found out from her calls to the hospitals.

At first, the man was speechless. Then he asked, "What business is it of yours?"

"My name is Klooz," I answered. "I want to know who told you this lie."

The man laughed. "You think you're pretty smart, Flooz. I'm not going to tell you a single thing."

I tried to stay cool. "The name is Klooz, not Flooz," I told him. "If you don't want to work with me, then I'll just talk to your boss. He would certainly be interested in how you write stories without checking the facts first."

For a moment it seemed as if the man would go for my throat. Then he pulled himself together.

"All right, little Flooz," the man mumbled. "It's nice when kids today are so curious. Someone from the police called me. His name was Peter Petersen. Why do you care?"

"I am a private detective," I replied.

I walked away and left the reporter sitting at his desk with his mouth hanging wide open.

Once I was outside, I went to the first phone booth I could find. I always had spare change for the pay phone with me. I really wanted a cell phone, but my mom wouldn't let me get one.

"Police station, Sergeant Sanger here," said the voice on the other end of the phone line.

"Hello. I would like to speak with Officer Petersen," I said.

"Who is that?" the policeman asked.

"He is a police officer there," I replied.

"There is no Officer Petersen here," he said.

"Are you sure?" I asked.

"One hundred percent," the man replied.

I hung up. I was deep in thought.

My last doubt was gone.

Someone was trying to mess with Odin and Bill the Mask.

But why? What had they done to deserve this?

There were so many dogs in the city. Why would someone choose to bother Odin?

I would find out, or my name wasn't Klooz.

CHAPTER 4

Bones and Poison

On Saturday morning I had breakfast with my mom. It was her day off.

My mom told me about things that had happened while she was working at the hospital.

I told her what I had found out from the newspaper and the police about Odin and the other, mysterious Great Dane.

After we cleared the table and washed the dishes, I headed to the city park.

I'm not sure what I was looking for there, but I had to continue working on my case somehow. The park seemed like the smartest place to go.

There was only one car parked in the parking lot. It was a station wagon that had a metal screen inside, separating the back of the car from the rest of it. It was one of those things that you could use to keep a dog in the back seat.

I hid behind a bush and waited for the car's owner to return.

At some point it started to rain and the water poured into the collar of my jacket.

After two hours, I was pretty soaked.

Just then, a man came walking out of the forest. He was wearing a long raincoat and a hat that was pulled down over his face.

He carelessly dropped a plastic bag by one of the trash cans.

Then he jumped into his car, and sped off really fast.

The guy was obviously in a hurry!

I came out from behind the bush and took a closer look at the plastic bag.

There was nothing unusual about it
from the outside, but inside I found a
bone. It looked like the ones Ms. Becker
buys to give to her dog.

Except this bone had an unusual
smell. In fact, it smelled terrible.

Hmm, I thought.

Why did the raincoat man bring a stinky bone into the park with him?

Could the bone be poisoned? And what if more of these things were lying around in the park? Did the man think Odin would be in the park later?

I spent the next few hours searching the park and the path that Bill the Mask and his dog had taken the day before.

I did find a few bones that smelled exactly like the one in the plastic bag.

I found something else, too. It was a dead fox.

It could have been a coincidence, but I was certain that the animal had been poisoned by one of the bones.

I took the bus to Bill the Mask's house. It took him a while to open the door. He was wearing a bathing suit, flip flops, and his usual hat.

"Come in, Klooz," he said. "Don't worry about the mess. I was up very late last night."

Odin greeted me inside. He placed his paws on my shoulders and would have tipped me over if Bill the Mask hadn't been standing next to me.

"Down, Odin," Bill the Mask said. The dog did what he was told.

It looked like a tornado had hit the house. There were papers and clothes everywhere.

Plates with leftover food were piled on the couch and end table.

Bill the Mask carelessly pushed a pair of pants and a sock from an easy chair and said, "Make yourself at home, Klooz. What's the news? Do you know who has it in for Odin and me?"

I shook my head. "I found this," I said. I held up the plastic bag.

Bill the Mask took it from my hand. "Bones?" he asked. Then he smelled it. "Rat poison," he mumbled. "Where did you get this?"

I told him. Bill the Mask fell into a deep silence. Odin lay down near Bill's feet on the carpet and looked at Bill carefully with his yellow eyes. His tail banged against the floor.

"That scumbag!" Bill the Mask said. "That dirty dog!"

"Do you happen to know the man in the raincoat?" I wanted to know.

He shook his head. "I don't have any idea, Klooz. Do you have a piece of gum for me?"

I gave him one. Then I tried to make the mysteries all add up.

"Do you have enemies?" I asked.

"Enemies? Me?" Bill the Mask laughed. "No way!"

"Do you have neighbors who don't like your dog?" I asked.

"No," he said. "Everyone likes him. I have to make sure that they don't spoil him."

I asked him about the car from the parking lot.

Bill the Mask just shook his head again. He didn't know the car.

"Now you're stuck, right?" he asked while scratching behind his dog's ears.

"Not at all," I lied.

I didn't have any idea how I was going to solve this case.

"I think you and Odin should stay out of the park for the next few days," I suggested.

"You are right," Bill the Mask said. "Maybe you didn't find all of the bones. I will call the city so they can warn other dog owners."

I stood up.

"Are you leaving already?" Bill asked.

"Yes," I said. "Keep an eye on Odin. I'll be in touch."

CHAPTER 5

From Pinschers to Great Danes

That evening when I was walking home, I discovered a poster attached to the big chestnut tree in front of our apartment building.

It said, "Giant Dog Show. The best dog breeds in the world, from Pinschers to Great Danes."

The dog show would take place the next day.

Tickets were free!

"From Pinschers to Great Danes" kept going through my head as I opened the door to our apartment building.

From Pinschers to Great Danes.

What if Odin was competing in the show? Maybe a competitor wanted to keep him away. The station wagon at the park's parking lot looked like it was built for a dog to ride in. What if the raincoat man also had a Great Dane and was worried his dog would lose to Odin?

Klooz, I said to myself, you are a pretty smart cookie.

Once I was in our living room I picked up the phone to call Bill the Mask. I was in luck. He was still home.

"Are you going to be in the dog show?" I asked excitedly.

On the other end of the line I heard laughing. "I'm not, but Odin is. But how do you know that? Do you have a crystal ball?"

I told him about my ideas.

"Yes!" Bill the Mask said when I was finished. "I think you're right. What should we do?"

"The raincoat man will try again," I replied.

"Yeah, he will," Bill the Mask said.

"So we have to catch him in the act," I continued. Then I explained my plan to him. "You need to keep an eye on Odin until I get there. After that, I'll take over."

"Okay, Klooz. But how are you going to get here?" Bill the Mask asked. "Your mom isn't just going to let you leave, is she?"

"That's no problem," I replied.

That night I put a pack of gum, a bottle of milk, a thick sweater, and a flashlight into my backpack.

Then I quietly opened the window and sat down on the windowsill. I climbed down the rain gutter and made it to the ground without hurting myself.

There wasn't much going on in the city at this time of night.

In the neighborhood where Bill the Mask lived, no one was outside. A light was on in Bill's little house.

When I rang the doorbell the man with the mask opened the door. Odin was standing beside him.

"Is everything all right?" I asked.

Bill the Mask nodded. "I haven't let him out of my sight."

"Bring him to his doghouse," I said. "It's my turn to watch him."

"No way, man!" Bill objected. "I'll keep watch with you. You're still a kid, after all."

I shrugged my shoulders. "Have it your way," I said.

We put Odin in the kennel behind the house and hid in the shadows of a tool shed. The dog paced back and forth for a while. Then he calmed down and lay down in a corner. Time passed.

"He isn't coming," Bill the Mask muttered. He yawned.

"He is coming," I said.

I don't know how I knew, but I knew he would.

After a while, I heard Bill the Mask breathing. He had fallen asleep.

If the man with the raincoat came, I could always wake Bill the Mask up.

It was long past midnight when a car without its headlights on rolled down the street. Brakes squeaked and a car door closed quietly.

My detective sense told me that this was it. I tried to wake up Bill the Mask, but he wouldn't move.

Great. Now I had to do it all myself.

The gate to the backyard squeaked. I could hear someone walking on gravel. I held my breath and looked around the corner of the tool shed.

The man with the raincoat and the hat pushed down over his face was creeping towards the kennel.

Then Odin woke up. He stood up and looked at the man, but he didn't growl or bark. The yellow eyes of the dog glowed with a ghostly light.

Then everything happened as quick as lightning. The man reached into his coat pocket.

I thought he wanted to shoot the dog. So I jumped up from my hiding place and tried to grab the man's arm.

Something wet flowed over my hand.

I tried to grab the man's coat, but the man shook me off and ran back to his car. The motor started and the car zipped away. It was a station wagon. I could see that even in the darkness.

The noise woke Bill the Mask. "What's going on?" he cried.

"He was here!" I called. "The man with the raincoat!"

"Nonsense," Bill the Mask growled. He rubbed his eyes. "You were just dreaming. Come inside the house!"

I suddenly noticed that my entire left hand was bright red.

"Now do you believe that the raincoat man was here?" I asked Bill the Mask. "He wanted to dye Odin. Then your dog couldn't have been in the dog show."

"Dye washes off," Bill the Mask said.

No matter how hard we scrubbed and rubbed, the red color stayed on my hand.

"If the man comes to the dog show we'll be able to catch him," I said. "The man definitely got some of the dye on himself, too. If we see someone with red dye on his hands, that's our man."

* * *

The next day it was hard to keep my hand hidden from my mom. At breakfast I kept my hand in my pocket.

She looked at me with a raised eyebrow, but didn't say anything.

Maybe she was too tired to have a talk about table manners. That was okay with me.

After breakfast, I went to the dog show. There wasn't much going on yet. A few dogs were waiting in their cages. Others were being brushed and combed by their owners.

Bill the Mask and Odin had not yet arrived.

I found a man near the dog kennels who was wearing gloves. It was as hot as a desert in the room and he was wearing gloves!

There was a Great Dane in the kennel he was about to open. The sign on the kennel read: Alf, four-time world champion. Thoughts raced through my head. What should I do?

Take it easy, I told myself as I stuck a piece of Carpenter's gum in my mouth.

I was certain that the man standing in front of that kennel had tried to get Odin. If I could take a look at his hands, I would have the proof.

I decided to walk over to the man. "Hello," I said. I held out my hand to shake his.

Instead of taking off his gloves like a polite person should and shaking my hand, he just nodded at me.

Then I saw it. He had a large red spot on his chin.

I knew I had him, but I didn't want to rush things.

"That's a good-looking dog," I said.

"Alf is the best," the man replied. "He's going to win again."

"No, he won't," I argued.

First the man looked at me. He seemed confused. Then he broke out in laughter.

That didn't sound good.

"Why not, little man?" he asked.

I stepped toward him and held my red fist in front of his face. "This is why," I said. "Last night you wanted to put dye on Odin. I knocked it out of your hand."

The man gulped.

"Take your dog right now and get lost, or I'll call the police," I said. "I think they'll be interested in the rat poison."

The man's eyes turned angry. "You . . . you . . . you . . ." he growled.

"My name is Klooz, and I am a detective," I said. "Now, get out of here!"

Of course Odin won the contest. He got the highest number of points that a Great Dane had ever gotten.

Bill the Mask almost cried when Odin got the trophy.

Odin licked my face to thank me.

My usual fee was doubled. Bill the Mask

bought me ten packs of Carpenter's gum.

I didn't have a problem with that.

A few days later, I was at Olga's newspaper stand. She took me aside.

"I have a case for you," she said.

A case? I was interested.

"My neighbor's dog ran away," Olga explained. "She wants to know if you will look for him. I told her that you're a dog expert."

I took a deep breath. "Olga!" I roared. "A serious detective doesn't look for dogs! Understand?"

"I understand," Olga said meekly. "How would you like a soda, sweetie?"

About the Author

Jürgen Banscherus is a worldwide phenomenon. There are almost a million Klooz books in print, and they have been translated into Spanish, Danish, Thai, Chinese, and eleven other languages. He has worked as a newspaper writer, a research scientist, and a teacher. His first book for children was published in 1985. He lives with his family in Germany.

About the Illustrator

Ralf Butschkow was born in Berlin. He works as a freelance graphic designer and illustrator, and has published more than 50 books for children. Critics have praised his work as "thoroughly enjoyable," "creatively original," and "highly recommended."

Glossary

coincidence (koh-IN-si-duhnss)—a chance happening

concentrate (KON-suhn-trate)—to focus your thoughts and attention on something

gigantic (ji-GAN-tik)—huge

Great Dane (GRATE DAYN)—a breed of dog (in this story, Odin is a Great Dane)

kennel (KEN-uhl)—a shelter where dogs and cats are kept

obedient (oh-BEE-dee-uhnt)—does what they are told

Pinscher (PINCH-uhr)—a breed of dog

reporter (ree-POR-tur)—someone who writes articles for a newspaper or magazine

suspicious (suh-SPISH-uhss)—thinking or feeling that something is wrong

transport (transs-PORT)—move around

Discussion Questions

1. Klooz says that he doesn't usually take dog cases, but this case is different. What is different about the Case of the Snarling Suspect? Why does he decide to take the case?

2. Bill the Mask's dog, Odin, is falsely accused of committing a crime. Have you ever been falsely accused of something? What did you do to prove that you were innocent? Talk about it.

3. How does Klooz solve the mystery? Talk about the clues he learns and how he finally puts everything together.

Writing Prompts

1. At the beginning of this book, Klooz is feeling bad about his ability as a detective. Have you ever felt discouraged about your ability to do something? What happened? Write about it.

2. Sometimes it can be interesting to imagine a story from another character's point of view. Try writing chapter 5 from Bill the Mask's point of view. What does he think about? What does he see and feel?

3. Klooz learns a lot from newspaper articles in this book. Write your own newspaper article describing the dog show and what had happened to Odin. Remember to give your article a headline!